W9-CTJ-037

Thumbelina

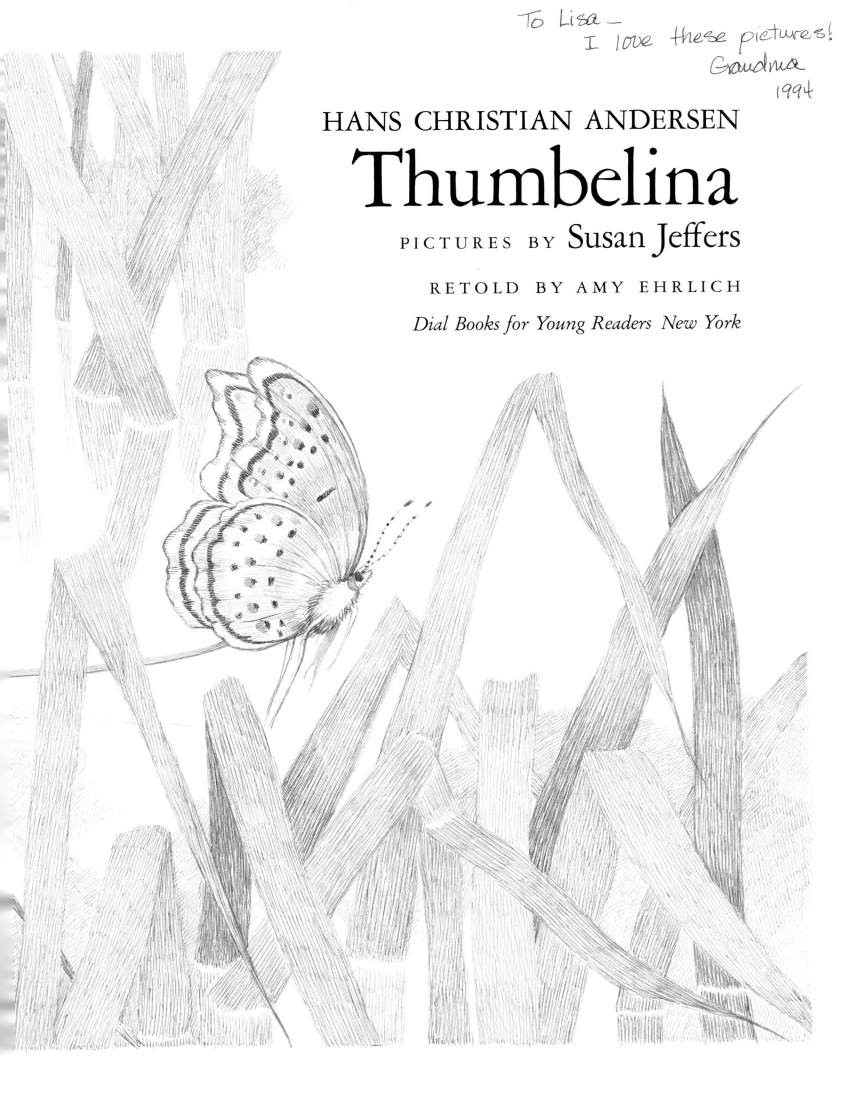

To Lisa —
I love these pictures!
Grandma
1994

HANS CHRISTIAN ANDERSEN

Thumbelina

PICTURES BY Susan Jeffers

RETOLD BY AMY EHRLICH

Dial Books for Young Readers New York

For Gabriele, Brent, and Karina

Dial Books for Young Readers
A Division of Penguin Books USA Inc.
375 Hudson Street
New York, New York 10014

Text copyright © 1979 by Amy Ehrlich
Pictures copyright © 1979 by Susan Jeffers
All rights reserved.
Library of Congress Catalog Card Number: 79-50146
Printed in Hong Kong by South China Printing Company (1988) Limited
First Pied Piper Printing 1985
COBE
4 5 6 7 8 9 10

A Pied Piper Book is a registered trademark of
Dial Books for Young Readers,
a division of Penguin Books USA Inc.,
® TM 1,163,686 and ® TM 1,054,312

THUMBELINA
is published in a hardcover edition by
Dial Books for Young Readers.
ISBN 0-8037-0232-9

*The full-color artwork was prepared using a fine-line
pen with ink and dyes. They were applied over a
detailed pencil drawing that was then erased.
The artwork was then camera-separated and reproduced
as red, blue, yellow, and black halftones.*

Once there was a woman who wanted a child more than anything in the world. At last in loneliness and sorrow she went to a witch and spoke of her desire.

"That's as easy as winking!" said the witch. "Take this seed and plant it in a flowerpot filled with good, rich earth. Water it carefully and guard it very well."

The woman did as the witch had said. The first time she watered the seed, a large and brilliant flower sprang up. It was still in bud, its petals tightly closed.

The woman bent to kiss the flower. But the moment her lips touched the silky petals, they began to open. The woman could not believe her eyes. There inside sat a tiny little girl. She was perfectly formed, as graceful as the flower from which she'd come. When the woman held her, she discovered that she was not even the size of her thumb.

Though she was a wonderful child in every way, she never grew at all. She was called Thumbelina and was treated with great extravagance and care. Her cradle was a polished walnut shell; each night she slept between fresh flower petals. In the daytime she liked to sit on a table and sing in the sunlight. Her voice was very beautiful—high and haunting and silvery.

One night as she lay sleeping, a toad hopped in at the window. "What a lovely wife for my son!" she said. Without even looking around her, she took up the walnut shell and hopped off with it to her home by the edge of a stream.

"Here, look what I brought you," said the toad proudly to her son. But the only sound he could utter was *"Koax, koax, brekke-ke-kex."*

"Don't talk so loud or you will wake her," complained the toad. "She might still run away from us, for she is light as swan's down."

Holding the walnut shell high, the toad swam out into the stream to an eddy where masses of water lilies grew. On a leaf far from shore she put the cradle. Then she went back to build a new room in the mud for the bride.

In the morning Thumbelina woke up and looked all around her at the great arching sky. She felt her cradle rock with the motion of the stream and cried out in terror.

The fish swimming in the water below came to the surface and looked curiously at Thumbelina. "Oh, please help me," she said. "I must get away from here."

And so the fish began to gnaw at the lily stalk with their sharp little teeth.

At last the leaf broke free and floated down the stream. Away went Thumbelina, gently spinning with the current. Gradually her fear left her, and she began to enjoy the journey. Never before had she been outside.

A beautiful butterfly flew near her. Fascinated by its gossamer wings, Thumbelina sat very still to show she meant no harm. The butterfly kept darting toward the sash on her dress, and Thumbelina thought to fasten one end loosely around it. She tied the other end to the stalk of the lily pad, and the butterfly flew along, pulling the lily pad behind like a little toy boat.

Thumbelina glided much faster now, but as night came on, she saw that the butterfly was growing weary. She called it to her and asked that it take her to shore. Gently she unfastened the sash. The butterfly hovered near her for a time, then slowly flew off. Thumbelina felt sad as she watched it disappear. Now she was truly alone, and the place was a foreign land to her.

The whole summer through Thumbelina lived by herself at the edge of the stream. She wove a bed of grass stems and hung it like a hammock under a large, spreading leaf to shelter herself from the rain. She sipped nectar from the flowers and drank the dew which lay on the leaves at dawn.

But when summer ended, the plants and flowers withered. The birds that had sung to her flew away, and there was frost on the ground each morning. Thumbelina's clothes were in rags, and she shivered with the cold. Autumn passed, and then one day it began to snow. Each snowflake fell like a veil upon her. She feared that she would be buried or that she would freeze to death. *Run!* she thought. She must run to find shelter.

The snow came at her in white swirling clouds, and she stumbled along until she came to a large cornfield. Suddenly she saw a hole that tunneled down into the earth. It would be warmer there perhaps and the snow would not reach her. But when Thumbelina ran toward the hole, a field mouse appeared before her. "Come," said the creature and beckoned her to follow.

As they descended into the tunnel, Thumbelina realized that she was in the snug, small home of the field mouse. Corn was piled up all around her, and its smell was in the air.

"Please," said Thumbelina, "could I have a bit of corn to eat?"

"You poor, dear thing!" the field mouse answered kindly. "You had better come into my room and have dinner with me."

The two got on well together, and after some days the field mouse invited Thumbelina to work for her and stay the winter. Late one evening she said to dust the floor and polish everything in the room until it shone. An important visitor was coming to call.

This was a mole who was very rich and wore a sleek velvet coat. But he was blind. He hated the sun and mocked all the creatures who lived outdoors. The field mouse, however, was impressed by the mole's riches. She told Thumbelina to sing for him and tell stories of her travels. As he listened to Thumbelina's beautiful voice, the mole fell in love with her.

The next time he came to visit, he said he would show them his rooms underground. By the pale light of a piece of torchwood, he led them through a long, twisting passage. Suddenly they came upon a swallow lying sprawled and dead in the passageway. Thumbelina felt very sorry for the swallow, but the mole kicked at him with his stumpy legs. "What a pitiful life to be a bird," he said. "A creature who does nothing all day but fly from branch to branch deserves to starve to death in winter."

Thumbelina said nothing, but at night she crept out of bed and wove a blanket of hay. Taking up some torchwood for a lantern, she carried the blanket to the dead bird so that he might lie comfortably on the cold ground.

"Good-bye, swallow," she said. "It might have been you who sang to me this summer when all the trees were green." She laid her head on his soft feathers for a moment, then darted back in fright. Something moved inside him with the slow, steady rhythm of a heartbeat. The bird was not dead; he was merely numbed with cold. The warmth of the blanket and of Thumbelina's body had stirred him back to life.

Each night after that she crept out of bed to tend the swallow. As he grew stronger, he told her how he had torn his wing on a thornbush. The other swallows had flown away to the warm countries, but he had not been able to keep up with them. At last he could go no farther and had plummeted to the ground.

Thumbelina cautioned him never to move from where he lay, for if the field mouse and the mole knew he was alive, they would surely kill him.

When spring warmed the earth once more, Thumbelina knew it was time for the swallow to go. His wing had healed now. Each night he fluttered it over and over again, strengthening it for flying. "Won't you come with me?" he asked her. "You can easily sit upon my back, and I will carry you away into the leafy woods."

But Thumbelina could not bring herself to abandon the field mouse who had kept her from starving. She made a hole in the roof of the passageway and watched longingly as the swallow flew out into the sunshine. She felt that all the pleasure in her life was going with him.

Every evening now the mole came to call on Thumbelina. He made her sing until her voice grew hoarse. Whenever she stopped, he prodded her to continue. This was the way he loved her. Without ever once asking Thumbelina, the mole and the field mouse agreed that she would be married to him in the autumn.

Suddenly there was a hum of activity in the field mouse's room, for she had insisted that the bride have a wardrobe of new clothes. Four spiders were hired to weave day and night, and Thumbelina was put to work spinning linen thread from flax. The mole felt it was all for him. He liked to sit in his chair and listen to the whirring sound of the spinning wheel.

But Thumbelina wept bitterly. Every morning when the sun rose and every evening when it set, she was allowed to go to the doorsill and stand outside. In the heat of August the corn had grown as high as a forest. When the wind blew the stalks apart, she could see bright pieces of sky. How beautiful it was! She did not know how she would live deep inside the earth with the mole whom she now despised more than ever.

As the time of her wedding drew closer, she sobbed out her fears to the field mouse. "Nonsense," the field mouse said. "Don't be stubborn or I'll bite you with my white teeth. His velvet coat is handsome, and the food in his pantry is fit for a queen."

Thumbelina understood then that she was trapped as surely as if she were in a cage. Summer was ending, and she knew she would never be able to survive outside through the harsh, cold months of winter.

But now the wedding day had come. For the last time she crept to the doorsill to stand in the sunshine. She knew the mole would never permit her to leave his side. She wept as she felt the warmth upon her face and made ready to go back into the earth. Then suddenly above her she heard a shower of notes, a glorious morning song.

She looked up, and there was the swallow.

"The cold winter is coming again," he said, flying down to her. "I've looked for you many times, and now I must fly away to the warm countries. Won't you come with me? I'll take you to where it is always summer."

This time Thumbelina did not hesitate. She climbed upon the swallow's back and tied her sash to one of his feathers. Then he rose up into the sky.

They flew over forests and fields, high above mountains with snowcapped peaks. When Thumbelina felt cold in the bleak air, she crept in under his feathers. It was so secure and close, a coverlet of softest down.

At last they arrived in the warm countries. The sun beat down upon the earth and the light was clear as crystal. Lemons and oranges hung on the trees and sweet spices perfumed the air.

The swallow flew on until they came to a dazzling white palace. In the pillars were many nests, and one of these was the swallow's home.

"I dearly love you and yearn to keep you with me," said the swallow sadly. "But I do not think you could live up high as I do, for when the wind comes, you might fall. Why don't you take one of the flowers that grows below for your home. At least we shall be neighbors."

Thumbelina did not remember that she had lived before in a flower, but the idea seemed to her a good one. The swallow set her gently on the petals of a brilliantly colored flower; then she slid inside.

But this could not be, she thought. The home was already taken!

A young man was standing there, shining as if he had been made of glass. A silver crown was on his head and gauzy wings grew from his back.

"Isn't he wonderful?" Thumbelina whispered to the swallow, who still hovered nearby. Never before had she seen a person just her size.

When the young man got over his fright at the closeness of the great bird, he explained to Thumbelina that a small person lived in each of the flowers; he was their king. Then he took off his crown and placed it upon Thumbelina's head. "You are so lovely," he said. "Won't you be my queen?"

Thumbelina never thought to refuse. She could tell he was kind by the sound of his voice and the curve of his mouth. She felt that at last she had come home.

Then the king declared that there was to be a welcoming party more joyful than any seen before in the land. From all the flowers men and women came, bringing gifts for Thumbelina. But the most wonderful was a pair of tiny wings that could be fastened to her back so she too could dart among the flowers. Everyone danced all night, and above them in his nest was the swallow, singing for them his most heartbreaking tune.